ISBN 978-1-331-75322-3
PIBN 10230294

This book is a reproduction of an important historical work. Forgotten Books uses
state-of-the-art technology to digitally reconstruct the work, preserving the original format
whilst repairing imperfections present in the aged copy. In rare cases, an imperfection in
the original, such as a blemish or missing page, may be replicated in our edition. We do,
however, repair the vast majority of imperfections successfully; any imperfections that
remain are intentionally left to preserve the state of such historical works.

1 MONTH OF
FREE
READING

at

www.ForgottenBooks.com

By purchasing this book you are eligible for one month membership to ForgottenBooks.com, giving you unlimited access to our entire collection of over 700,000 titles via our web site and mobile apps.

To claim your free month visit: www.forgottenbooks.com/free230294

THE

SUN-FLOWER;

OR

POETICAL BLOSSOMS.

Like as the Sun-Flower spreads its leaves
To meet the Sun's bright rays,
The youthful mind with warmth receives
The moral Truth conveys.

NEW HAVEN.
PRINTED AND PUBLISHED
BY S. BABCOCK.

THE

SUN-FLOWER;

OR

POETICAL BLOSSOMS.

Like as the Sun-Flower spreads its leaves
To meet the Sun's bright rays,
The youthful mind with warmth receives
The moral Truth conveys.

NEW HAVEN,

PRINTED AND PUBLISHED

BY S. BABCOCK.

THE

SUN-FLOWER.

ANN AND THE CAT.

I like little pussy,
   Her coat is so warm;
And if I don't hurt her
   She'll do me no harm.

So I'll not pull her tail,
   Nor drive her away,
But pussy and I
   Very gently will play.

She shall sit by my side,
   And I'll give her some food,
And she'll love me, because
   I am gentle and good.

THE GOOD SCHOLAR.

Henry Banks, though very young,
Will never do what's rude or wrong;
When spoken to, he always tries
To give the most polite replies.

Observing what at school he's taught,
He minds his books, as children ought,
And when return'd at night from
    school,
He never lolls on chair or stool.

Some children, when they write, we
    know,
Their ink about them, heedless, throw;
But he, though young, has learned to
    think
That clothes look spoiled with spots
    of ink.

Perhaps some little boy may ask,
If Henry always learns his task;
With pleasure I can answer this,
Because with truth I answer, "Yes."

THE SUN-FLOWER.

THE NEW PENNY.

Little Ann saw a man
Quite poor at the door,
And Ann had a pretty new penny,
Now this the kind girl
Threw pat in his hat,
Although she was left without any.

She meant, as she went,
To stop at a shop,
Where cakes she had seen a great
    many,
And buy a fruit pie,
Or take home a cake
By spending her pretty new penny.

But well I can tell,
When Ann gave the man
Her money, she wished not for any;
He said, " I've no bread,"
Ann heard, and preferred
To give him her pretty new penny.

IMPROVEMENT.

Another story, mother dear,
  Did young Maria say ;
You read so nice, so loud and clear,—
  Another story, pray.

I love that book, I do indeed,
  So take it up again ;
I think I *see* the things you read,
  You make it all so plain.

What would I give to read like you.
  Why nothing comes amiss!
O, any thing I'll gladly do,
  If you will teach me this.

Maria, then, must learn to spell,
  If she would read like me ;
She soon may learn to read as well ;
  O, that I will, said she.

Young readers, it is truth I speak,
  Such pains she daily took,
In rather better than one week,
  She learned to read this book.

CLEVER LITTLE THOMAS.

When Thomas Poole
First went to school,
He was but scarcely seven;
Yet knew as well
To read and spell
As most boys of eleven.

He took his seat,
And wrote quite neat,
And never idly acted;
And then, beside,
He multiplied,
Divided and subtracted

His master said,
(And stroked his head)
"If thus you persevere,
My little friend,
You may depend
Upon a Prize next year."

THE LETTER.

When Mary's papa was from home a
    great way,
She attempted to write him a letter
    one day,
So ruling the paper, an excellent plan,
In all proper order, little Mary began.

She wrote, she lamented sincerely to
    tell,
That her dearest mamma had been
    very unwell;
That her story was long, but when he
    came back,
He would hear of the shocking beha-
    vior of Jack.

Though an error or two we by chance
    may detect,
It was better than treating papa with
    neglect,
For Mary, when older, we know will
    learn better,
And write her papa a most excellent
    letter.

EVENING HYMN.

And now another day is gone,
   I'll sing my Maker's praise ;
My comforts ev'ry hour make known
   His providence and grace.

But how my childhood runs to waste!
   My sins how great their sum !
Lord, give me pardon for the past,
   And strength for days to come.

I lay my body down to sleep ;
   Let angels guard my head ;
And thro' the hours of darkness keep
   Their watch around my bed.

With cheerful heart I close mine eyes,
   Since thou wilt not remove ;
And in the morning let me rise,
   Rejoicing in thy love.

THE TEAR

What was it dropp'd upon my cheek?
  A tear from Anna's eye;
Lift up thy head, my love, and speak,
  Come, tell thy mother why?

It did not seem like passion's tear,
  Nor did it whim betray;
A better dress it seem'd to wear;
  And gently forc'd its way.

Her linnet's death makes Anna dull,
  She saw it droop and die;
The grief which found her heart too
      full,
  Took shelter in her eye.

Then not for worlds I'll check its
      course,
  Too dear the gem I hold;
The tear that springs from pity's
      source,
  Is worth a mine of gold.

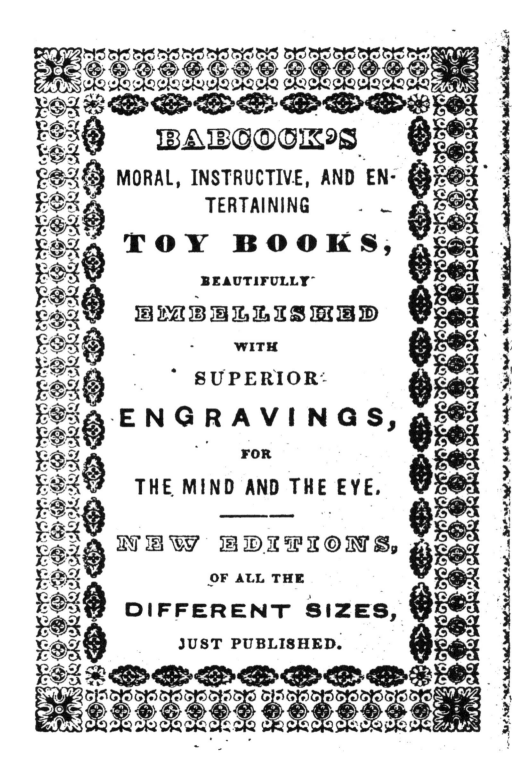

BABCOCK'S

MORAL, INSTRUCTIVE, AND EN-TERTAINING

TOY BOOKS,

BEAUTIFULLY

EMBELLISHED

WITH

SUPERIOR

ENGRAVINGS,

FOR

THE MIND AND THE EYE.

NEW EDITIONS,

OF ALL THE

DIFFERENT SIZES,

JUST PUBLISHED.

CPSIA information can be obtained
at www.ICGtesting.com
Printed in the USA
BVHW041103211218
536078BV00026B/378/P

9 781331 753223